For Neil and Lizzy
With love M.B.

JESSICA STRANGE
by Malorie Blackman. Illustrated by Alison Bartlett
British Library Cataloguing in Publication Data
A catalogue record of this book is available from the British Library.

ISBN 0 340 77963 2 (HB)
ISBN 0 340 77964 0 (PB)

Text copyright © Malorie Blackman 2002
Illustrations copyright © Alison Bartlett 2002

The right of Malorie Blackman to be identified as the author of this Work
and of Alison Bartlett to be identified as the illustrator of this Work
has been asserted by them in accordance with
the Copyright, Designs and Patents Act 1988.

First edition published 2002
10 9 8 7 6 5 4 3

Published by Hodder Children's Books
a division of Hodder Headline Limited
338 Euston Road, London NW1 3BH

Printed in Hong Kong

Jessica Strange

Malorie Blackman • Alison Bartlett

*Hodder
Children's
Books*

A division of Hodder Headline Limited

J essica Strange didn't look like her brothers
and sisters.

In fact, Jessica looked so different from the rest
of her family that she began to wonder what she was.

"Jessica, you're a beautiful mouse, even if you are rather big!" said her mum.

"I don't think I am a mouse, Mum," said Jessica, doubtfully.

"Darling, of course you're a mouse. Go and ask the other animals around the farm if you don't believe me," said her mum.

So Jessica decided to do just that.

As she set off across the farmyard,
a butterfly fluttered by.

"Excuse me, Madam Butterfly," Jessica began.
"What kind of animal do you think I am?"

"Well, you've got four legs... so you must be
a cow," Madam Butterfly decided.

And off she flew.

"Excuse me, Mrs Cow," said Jessica. "But what kind of animal am I?"

Mrs Cow looked down. "You're very small, so you must be an ant."

An ant? Jessica left the meadow.

"Excuse me, Ant sir," asked Jessica. "But could you take a good look at me and tell me what kind of animal you think I am?"

The ant took a long, hard look. "You're very, very big so I'd have to say you're a horse."

A horse? Jessica ran across to the stables.

"Hello there, Captain," Jessica said politely. "I'm sorry to disturb you but I'd like to ask you a question. What type of creature am I?"

"Don't you know?" asked Captain.

"Well, everyone seems to have different views about it," said Jessica.

"Well, you've got big yellow eyes, so you must be an owl."

An owl? Jessica climbed up the tall tree by the pond.

"Excuse me, Mrs Owl," said Jessica. "But what kind of animal do I look like to you?"

Mrs Owl opened one eye, looking very cross indeed. She blinked, then blinked again.

"You've got a long tail, so I reckon you're a dog," Mrs Owl said at last. "Now let me get some sleep!"

A dog? Jessica jumped down from the tree and raced over to the kennel.

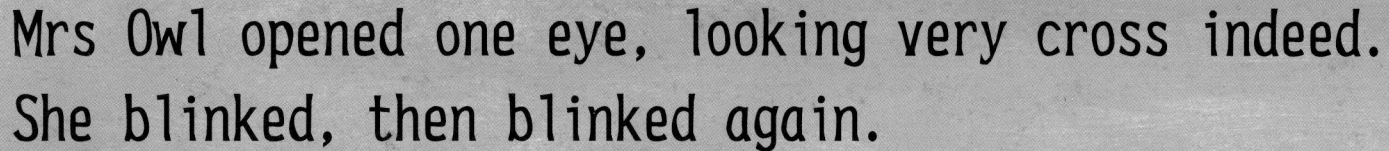

"Larry, I need your help," said Jessica.
"Am I a dog?"

"Of course not. You're soft and fluffy so you must be a duckling!"

A duckling? Jessica was feeling quite sad by now.
No one seemed to know what she was.
She walked over to the
duck pond.

"Mrs Duck, am I a duckling?"

Mrs Duck thought long and hard before answering. "What do you want to be?"

"Well, I'm not a butterfly, or a cow, or an ant, or a horse, or an owl, or a dog. I want to be a mouse, but I think I'm a cat," Jessica admitted.

"Why do you want to be a mouse?"

"So I can stay with my brothers and sisters for ever," said Jessica.

"I see. And why do you think you're a cat?"

"Because I don't look like my brothers and sisters. My whiskers are longer and my eyes are bigger and my fur is thicker and my tail is furrier and my teeth are sharper," said Jessica.

"So what?" said Mrs Duck. "If you want to stay with your brothers and sisters, then stay with them. It doesn't matter what you are, as long as you love them and they love you."

"It really doesn't matter?" asked Jessica surprised.

"Of course it doesn't," smiled Mrs Duck.

"Then I'll just be Jessica Strange," Jessica decided.

And she trotted back home, just in time for a game of chase before dinner.